Stop That Poodnoobie!

The bug had started to fly down the aisle. But Lunk was interested in it now. He followed after it. More destruction.

The bug began flying in circles at the front of the room.

Lunk began leaping after it.

Badoom! Badoom! Badoom! The floor shook with each leap as desks and children began bouncing into the air.

"Blork!" cried Modra Ploogsik. "Stop that poodnoobie!"

Books by Bruce Coville

The A.I. Gang Trilogy
    Operation Sherlock
    Robot Trouble
    Forever Begins Tomorrow

Bruce Coville's Alien Adventures
    Aliens Ate My Homework
    I Left My Sneakers in Dimension X
    The Search for Snout
    Aliens Stole My Body

Camp Haunted Hills
    How I Survived My Summer Vacation
    Some of My Best Friends Are Monsters
    The Dinosaur That Followed Me Home

I Was a Sixth Grade Alien
    I Was a Sixth Grade Alien
    The Attack of the Two-Inch Teacher
    I Lost My Grandfather's Brain
    Peanut Butter Lover Boy
    Zombies of the Science Fair
    Don't Fry My Veeblax!
    Too Many Aliens
    Snatched from Earth
    There's an Alien in My Backpack
    The Revolt of the Miniature Mutants

Magic Shop Books
    Jennifer Murdley's Toad
    Jeremy Thatcher, Dragon Hatcher
    The Monster's Ring
    The Skull of Truth

My Teacher Books
    My Teacher Is an Alien
    My Teacher Fried My Brains
    My Teacher Glows in the Dark
    My Teacher Flunked the Planet

BRUCE COVILLE

Interior illustrations by
Katherine Coville

Aladdin Paperbacks
New York   London   Toronto   Sydney   Singapore

First Aladdin Paperbacks edition May 2002

Originally published in 1992 by Minstrel® Paperbacks

ALADDIN PAPERBACKS
An imprint of Simon & Schuster
Children's Publishing Division
1230 Avenue of the Americas
New York, NY 10020

Printed in the U.S.A.
12 14 16 18 20 19 17 15 13 11

ISBN: 0-671-74567-0

For our own three brats,
who kept wanting to know why
this wasn't a book.
Now it is.

Contents

1

BLORK

Blork was sitting in his secret place, holding his poodnoobie.

It's not easy to hold a poodnoobie. They have six legs, are covered with purple fur, and weigh about three hundred and fifty pounds. But they like to be held, and Blork always felt better when he held this one. So it worked out very nicely.

The reason Blork was holding his poodnoo-bie and trying to feel better was that he had just had a tantrum.

That was not unusual. Blork had tantrums a lot.

Only this tantrum hadn't worked. That *was* unusual, and Blork was crushed.

Blork had tantrums for two reasons.

First, he had learned a long time ago that having a tantrum would almost always get him his own way.

Second, he had been having them so long that it had gotten to be a habit.

Today's tantrum had started because Blork's teacher, Modra Ploogsik, had given him a D in geography. Blork wanted it changed. But since the D was already in the class computer, and computers don't care about tantrums, his efforts had been wasted.

Now Blork felt really rotten. "Nobody loves me," he said to Lunk. Lunk stuck out one of his long green tongues (poodnoobies have three of them) and licked Blork's face. He used the smooth tongue, which felt nice.

"Well, maybe *you* love me," said Blork. "But no one else does."

Basically that was true. No one did love Blork.

But then, Blork was not very lovable.

It wasn't really Blork's fault he was so un-lovable. In fact, he had become a brat by accident.

Here's how it happened:

On the Planet Splat children are hatched instead of being born. They sleep very quietly for about three months. Then they get up and start to walk and are fun to play with.

This system suits the grown-ups very well.

Unfortunately, when Blork came out of his egg, a piece of shell got stuck behind his ear. It hurt. Blork began to cry.

Children on Splat are not expected to cry.

The robot in charge of Blork's nursery came rolling over and stuck a label on his forehead.

BRAT, it said, in big black letters.

That was how it all began. Eventually the piece of eggshell fell away, and Blork was no longer in pain. But because he never did get the normal amount of sleep for a Splatoon baby, he was always slightly cranky.

Even worse, since he had a brat label on his forehead, everyone expected him to *be* a brat.

This meant that Blork got blamed for everything.

Now, children are never perfect, even on Splat. But some grown-ups like to think they are. So whenever anything went wrong, the grown-ups would blame it on Blork. That way they could go on thinking that the rest of the kids were perfect.

This meant that when Appus Meko glued the eyes shut on all the dolls in the Block 78 Child House, it was Blork who got sent to the Whacking Room.

When Murgo put an extra dose of plant food in the principal's Bongoo plant, causing it to take over the office, the hallway, and two classrooms, it was Blork who had to write "I will not feed the plants unless asked" 500,000 times.

And when Lakka found a used laser with a little bit of charge left in it, and carved a *very* bad word in the school wall, it was Blork who had to spend three weeks in the Big Black Pit.

(One reason children on Splat tend to be well behaved is that the punishments are rather strict.)

Blork was sick of being punished for things he didn't do. He decided if he was going to be punished so often, he might as well go ahead and do something bad. But before he got a chance, there was another disaster. Someone put antigravity powder in Modra Ploogsik's lunch. It was late afternoon before they finally got her off the ceiling.

When Blork was blamed, he felt something snap inside of him. He began to cry.

Everyone stepped back.

He began to scream.

A murmur of amazement rippled through the classroom.

He began to kick and holler.

Someone went to get the principal.

Soon Blork was bouncing up and down. He bit a chair. He held his breath until he turned blue. Finally he flopped onto his stomach and began pounding the floor with his hands and feet.

The principal sent for the Head Man—which is what the Splatoons call someone who takes care of head problems.

The Head Man took one look at Blork and said, "This child has been mismanaged. He needs a different treatment. From now on be more sympathetic. Then he'll improve. I'm sure of it."

So Blork was not punished for the antigravity matter—which was just as well, because he hadn't done it. But he was not punished for anything else, either.

That was not so good, because he had made up his mind that he was going to do whatever he felt like.

Soon no one was safe from Blork and his tricks. One day he glued all the other kids to their seats with three-hour power-powder. At the end of the three hours they were so mad they would have turned *Blork* into powder, no matter what the Head Man said, if Blork had not had the good sense to be long gone.

Now poor Modra Ploogsik was not perfect. So even though the Head Man had told her not to, she sometimes lost her temper and threatened to punish Blork. This happened about every third time Blork did something really bad. But as soon as Modra Ploogsik said anything about punishment, Blork would have a fierce tantrum. Then the teacher would remember the Head Man's advice and leave Blork alone.

So Blork got worse and worse.

One thing got better: his tantrums. *They* were fantastic. Blork had the best tantrums on the Planet Splat. In fact, there were those who thought he probably had the best tantrums in the planetary system, or even the galaxy.

Yet, as effective as Blork's tantrums were, they did not impress the computer. Which was why Blork still had a D, despite his tantrum, and why he was feeling particularly bad at this moment, despite his poodnoobie.

Suddenly Blork made up his mind. If he couldn't get his way, he would get revenge.

"Lunk," he said, looking the poodnoobie in the eye, "you're coming to school with me tomorrow."

Lunk licked his face. Poodnoobies are lovable that way.

They are also big.

They are also exceedingly stupid.

Blork knew this very well.

He smiled.

Tomorrow should be very interesting.

2

LUNK

Blork was walking from the Block 78 Child House to school, whistling and kicking pebbles.

Lunk was walking beside him, drooling and burping, as poodnoobies tend to do.

Blork put out his hand and patted Lunk fondly.

He had found Lunk about three years ago, after a particularly bad day at school. On that morning he had gotten up feeling, as usual, slightly cranky. Then they had served Florjel Eggs for breakfast at the Child House.

Blork hated Florjel Eggs. They were brown on the inside, looked like mud, and tasted worse. When scrambled they were absolutely revolting. He had refused to eat them.

When the Childkeeper had rolled over to see what was wrong, Blork had told it, "If I eat these, I will throw up."

Since this was before his tantrum days, the Childkeeper had refused to give him anything else. So Blork had gone to school hungry.

Then he had failed a history test because he forgot the date when the first spaceships landed on Splat.

Then Appus Meko had picked on him because . . . well, basically because Appus Meko picked on everyone.

And finally he had lost his writing stick, and no one would loan him one because he had been so cranky all day. So Modra Ploogsik had made him stay after school to finish his work.

When Blork left school, Appus Meko and a group of his friends were waiting outside the door. They teased Blork and made jokes about staying after school. Their laughter hurt. Blork felt a tear begin to form in the corner of his eye. He hated crying, and he refused to do it in front of anyone.

He began to run. He ran as fast and as far as he could, beyond the school grounds, beyond the Block 78 Child House, beyond the edge of the city—all the way to the bubbling swamp that was marked with big OFF-LIMITS and DANGER signs.

Blork didn't care about the signs. He just wanted to get away from everyone and everything that had ever made his life miserable. Because he wasn't looking where he was going, he ran smack into a Roobkis plant. The stalk, which was bigger around than he was, snapped in half. It fell into the bubbling swamp and disappeared.

Blork sat down and rubbed his head.

Then he let out a shout. He could hardly believe his eyes. Inside the base of the stalk was a poodnoobie nest. Inside the nest was an egg!

Blork wrinkled his brow. He knew pood-noobies always laid their eggs in batches of four. Where were the others?

He looked again. Lying beside the egg were

three broken shells. He sighed. That meant this egg was no good. Poodnoobie eggs are all supposed to hatch at the same time. Then the mother, who is waiting outside the stalk, takes the babies off to raise them. The mother must have given up waiting for this egg and gone off with her other babies.

Blork glared at the egg. He hated it. He hated eggs in general, and he hated this one in particular because it shouldn't even be an egg. It should be a poodnoobie. Feeling spiteful, he picked up the egg and threw it against a rock.

The egg split open. Out rolled a little tiny poodnoobie.

Blork felt awful. He had had no idea there was something inside. He hoped it was all right.

He ran to the poodnoobie and picked it up. It was alive!

The poodnoobie just fit in the palm of Blork's hand. Its purple fur was soft and warm. Nestling against the curve of his fingers, it burped and went on sleeping.

Blork smiled for the first time that day.

Then he slipped the poodnoobie into the front of his jacket and headed for the Child House.

"But poodnoobies get so big!" said the Childkeeper.

It didn't know what to do. The rules stated that every child was allowed to have a pet, as long as he took care of it and cleaned up after it.

Blork knew the rules very well. The Childkeeper was stuck.

Blork named the poodnoobie Lunk and kept it in his room. He took very good care of it and fed it every day. And, as expected, the poodnoobie grew . . . and grew . . . and grew!

Which was just what Blork had wanted it to do.

And now he was on his way to school with a 350-pound, none-too-bright poodnoobie and smiling at the thought of what might happen.

At school Blork positioned the poodnoobie outside the door, then went quietly to take his seat. Modra Ploogsik called the class to order, took attendance, and asked who had something for Bring-and-Brag Time.

Blork raised his hand.

Modra Ploogsik raised an eyebrow. Blork rarely brought anything to show. When he did, it was usually dangerous. "What do you have, Blork?" she asked warily.

"My best friend," said Blork. Then he walked to the door at the back of the classroom and opened it.

Lunk waddled in, snorting and slurping. Blork led his pet between two rows of desks. But Lunk was a little too wide to fit, and his rear end knocked over all the desks.

Blork pretended not to notice. Lunk really didn't notice.

Modra Ploogsik was on her feet, her eyes

blazing. She opened her mouth, but nothing came out because she couldn't decide what to say first.

Blork looked back at the classroom. He pretended to be slightly startled at the sight of the overturned desks.

"Blork!" yelled Modra Ploogsik at last. "What do you think you're doing?"

"Showing you my poodnoobie," said Blork without a trace of a smile.

"Well, it doesn't belong here!"

Blork put his hands over Lunk's ears. "Shhh! You'll hurt his feelings!"

Modra Ploogsik began to tap her foot in a way that usually meant big trouble.

Blork replied with a pout. Sticking out his lower lip, he let it tremble a bit. "This poodnoobie is my best friend," he said. "You told us Bring-and-Brag should always be something close to us. Nothing is closer to me than Lunk."

Lunk stuck out his middle tongue, the medium rough one, and licked Blork's face.

"Well, he is kind of cute," said the teacher.

Lunk burped.

Blork went back to his seat. Lunk followed, knocking over three more desks in the process.

Things were quiet for a while, until Lunk noticed a small bug flying around his head. He tried to catch it with his middle tongue.

TOO MANY WRONG ANSWERS
TOO MANY RIGHT ANSWERS
LAUNCH GAS PELLETS
BIG BLACK PIT
LEARN

"Oooh!" cried Moomie Peevik, who was sitting next to Blork. "Lunk got slobber on my work! Yuk!"

"He can't help it!" cried Blork. "It's just the way he is."

The bug had started to fly down the aisle.

But Lunk was interested in it now. He followed after it. More destruction.

The bug began flying in circles at the front of the room.

Lunk began leaping after it.

Badoom! Badoom! Badoom! The floor shook with each leap as desks and children began bouncing into the air.

"Blork!" cried Modra Ploogsik. "Stop that poodnoobie!"

"Yes, ma'am," said Blork. He began to walk toward the front of the room.

Badoom!

Blork, and everything else in the room, bounced.

He took another step.

Badoom!

Bounce.

Badoom!

Bounce.

Blork was nearly there.

Unfortunately, the bug was heading for Modra Ploogsik's desk. Lunk followed, gaining speed with every mighty leap. He jumped onto the teacher's chair, and from there to her desk, where he stood, snapping at the bug, for about three seconds. Then the desk split beneath him. Its legs splayed out to both sides. Papers, pencils, erasers, and homework flew in all directions.

Blork stopped dead in his tracks. Revenge was one thing, but this had gotten out of hand. Trouble was coming.

He geared himself up for a tantrum.

Modra Ploogsik was shaking with rage. The poodnoobie was licking its front paw. The class was in a total uproar.

The teacher gave Blork a black look and stepped to the vidcom.

Tantrum-time, thought Blork.

He threw himself to the floor and began to scream.

The tantrum was a dilly. Even the kids who had seen him do this many times before were impressed. But Modra Ploogsik had been pushed too far. Punching a number into the vidcom, she said, very clearly, "Give me the Big Pest Squad."

Blork stopped in mid-kick. The Big Pest Squad! He knew what *they* did to poodnoobies. The same thing they did with other animals that got in the way or caused trouble.

They turned them into dust.

Dust!

Blork shivered. He couldn't let that happen to Lunk!

3

ESCAPE

The Big Pest Squad pulled up outside the school. Three men rushed in with big nets. They scooped Lunk into the nets and carried him out the door.

"*Lunk!*" cried Blork. He didn't know what to do. A tantrum wouldn't help now.

"Blork, sit down," said Modra Ploogsik. Blork didn't sit. He ran for the door.

Outside, he saw the men loading Lunk into a big rocket van.

"Stop!" cried Blork. "That poodnoobie belongs to me! I love him!"

The men paid no attention. After slamming the door on the back of the van, they jumped in front. In a second they would lift off. Lunk would be gone.

Blork climbed onto the back of the van. He didn't know what else to do. The rocket van gave a roar and leapt into the air.

Blork held on for dear life. After a minute he looked down. That was a mistake. He closed his eyes and tightened his grip on the van.

A short time later the rocket van landed in the center of the Big Pest Compound. As the men were climbing out of the front, Blork scrambled down from the back. Scuttling underneath, he watched the men's legs. Soon they were at the back of the van themselves.

Blork heard the doors open. Then he heard the sound of Lunk whimpering as the men dragged him through the doors.

Blork set his jaw. He had gotten Lunk into this. He would have to get him out. He felt a great surge of anger. Nothing in his life had ever worked out right. Now the only thing he really loved was going to be destroyed. He couldn't stand it. He wanted to get Lunk, then get away from everyone and everything.

Get away . . .

That started him thinking.

Blork crawled to the edge of the van and peeked out. He saw a rocket car on the other side of the compound. It was big and fancy. Probably it belonged to the chief of the Big Pest Squad. Blork was sure it would be equipped for a long flight.

BIG PEST
VAPORIZATION
FACILITY

YOU GOT EM
WE SPLOTTEM

EST SO

Slipping out from under the van, he ran for the rocket car.

A glance over his shoulder showed him that the men dragging Lunk across the compound had almost reached the building. He didn't have much time.

Leaping into the rocket car, Blork pushed the START button. The engines roared. The men carrying Lunk whirled around to see what was happening. As they did, Blork put the car into action. It lifted from the ground and soared across the compound.

The men took one look at what was coming, dropped Lunk, and ran for shelter. Blork found a button marked NET. Since the car belonged to the Big Pest Squad, he was pretty sure what the button would do. Zooming toward Lunk, he pushed it. A hatch opened in the bottom of the car. A net dropped out and scooped up Lunk.

Blork pulled back on the altitude control. The car soared into the air.

Now all he had to do was get Lunk inside—and decide where they were going next.

He flew farther up and put the car on automatic. The men from the Big Pest Squad would be after them soon. He was going to have to move fast.

He searched the control panel for a button that would bring Lunk back into the car. He couldn't find any that he was sure would bring the net in *before* opening it.

He didn't dare take a chance of dropping Lunk to the ground so far below. Finally he went to the back of the car. Flopping onto his stomach, he looked through the hatch.

Lunk dangled about ten feet below him. Thousands of feet below Lunk was the ground.

Blork felt his stomach lurch.

Lunk was whining and shaking.

Blork didn't blame him. "Don't worry, Lunkie," he said. "I'll get you back up here. Just close your eyes and hold on."

Lunk closed his eyes. But he continued to whine and shiver.

Blork racked his brains. What could he do?

Then he remembered a toy he had played with when he was younger—a ball on a string, attached to a cup at the end of a stick. If you made the right moves fast enough, you could get the cup under the ball and catch it.

Blork had gotten very good with that toy. He looked at the hole in the bottom of the car again. He wondered if he was good enough to do what he had in mind now.

He wasn't certain. But he had no choice.

Blork ran back to the control panel. He stared at it for a moment, then jammed the accelerator forward. At the same time he pushed a lever that made the car's path curve downward. Soon they were heading straight for the ground. But Blork kept the lever pressed forward. Instead of crashing, the car continued to curve, until it had made a perfect half circle. Now the car was flying completely upside down.

Plop!

Blork let out a cheer. Lunk had dropped right through the hole in the floor (which was now the ceiling). But they couldn't relax yet; he still had to get Lunk out of the net.

He continued to press the lever. The car's path continued to curve. Soon they were heading up again. Now Lunk's net was dan-

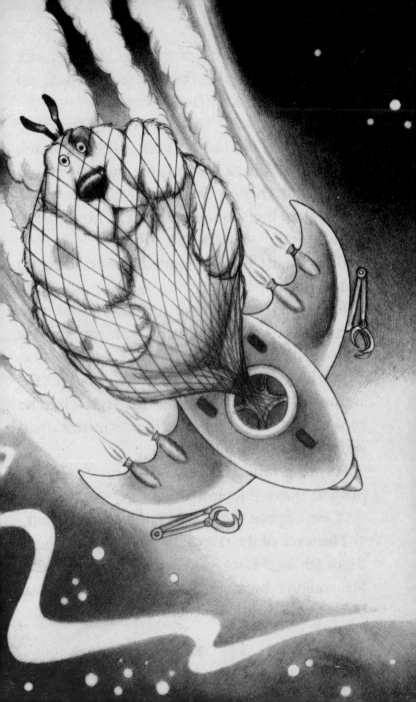

gling toward the back of the car. Finally Blork completed the circle. They were right side up again, with Lunk safely on the floor.

"We did it, boy!" cried Blork. "You're safe!"

He pressed the button that closed the hatch door and ran back to let Lunk out of the net.

Lunk licked Blork's face.

But they had no time to relax. The Big Pest Squad would soon be after them.

Blork made up his mind. He was going to run away.

For a Splatoon, that meant one of two things: A) the Unexplored Zone on the far side of Splat, or B) Deep Space.

Blork knew where he was going. He strapped Lunk into a cushioned seat. Then he took his place behind the controls and strapped himself in, too.

Pointing the car away from Splat, he pushed the accelerator.

"Deep Space, here we come!" he shouted.

The force of the takeoff began to squash them. Blork felt as if Lunk were sitting on top of him. He couldn't breathe. The skin of his face was being pushed down around his ears.

He wondered what he looked like, then decided he didn't want to know. He tried to sneak a look at Lunk, instead. He thought it would be interesting to see a poodnoobie being flattened. But the pressure was so strong he couldn't turn his head, no matter how hard he tried.

The pressure lasted only a short time. Soon they broke free of Splat's gravitational field.

They had done it! They were in space!

Blork unbuckled his seat belt and drifted into the air. Then he undid Lunk and gave him a tug. When he let go, the poodnoobie floated up to the roof of the car.

Lunk's eyes went wide with astonishment. Panic struck. He stuck out all three tongues at once and tried to run, which resulted in his feet making a ridiculous paddling motion in the air.

Blork laughed. "It's all right, Lunkie. You're safe from the Big Pest Squad now."

Lunk smiled and drooled.

Blork took the controls of the car.

Time went on.

Blork began to get bored. Being in space

was not as exciting as he had thought it would be. He began to understand why it was called space. That's all there was. Space.

A lot of emptiness.

Nothing.

Blork yawned and began to nod.

Soon he was asleep.

And the spaceship flew on.

4

SQUAT

Blork was worried.

His original plan had been to fly straight out from Splat. That way if he decided he wanted to go home, he could just turn around and fly straight back. But somewhere along the way he had gotten turned around. Now he had no idea where they were.

To make things worse, Lunk was getting bored. Bored poodnoobies were dangerous.

Worst of all, the rocket car was running out of food.

Blork did not want to be lost in Deep Space with a bored, hungry poodnoobie.

On their sixth day in the rocket car, Blork was sitting in the driver's seat, fiddling with the controls. The ship had a gravity field, and he had been turning it off and on, watching Lunk smack into the floor and then float back up to the ceiling again. It wasn't very nice, but it was the only thing he could think of to do.

Suddenly he spotted something ahead of them. "Hey, Lunkie!" he yelled. "Look. A planet!"

Lunk waddled over to where Blork stood.

"See," said Blork, pointing at the view screen. "Over that way. Maybe we can find some food there. Let's head for it."

Lunk drooled happily. He was sick of this spaceship.

Soon they were swooping over the surface of the planet. It looked strangely familiar to Blork. He shrugged. He must have seen it in one of his schoolbooks. He wished he had paid more attention in astronomy. If he had, maybe they wouldn't be lost now!

Dropping lower, Blork spotted a carefully tended field. Someone must be growing food there.

That was all he needed to see. Landing the ship, Blork and Lunk climbed out. They trotted to the field. It was filled with big purple plants. Blork was wearing a purple suit. Lunk had purple fur. They fit right in.

Then Blork noticed the people.

Well, *people* wasn't quite the right word. These were—Things. Each was about three times as tall as Blork, with broad shoulders

and long arms that hung down below its knees. Their pebbly skin was grayish-green. They had broad brows jutting out over their little eyes, flat noses, and two pointy teeth that stuck up from the bottoms of their mouths.

Blork shivered.

"We'd better get something to eat and go," he whispered to Lunk. He looked at the plants. Large purple globes hung from their upper stems. Blork poked one. It was soft. He wondered what it would taste like. He was reaching up to pick one when a huge hand grabbed him from behind.

"Hey!" yelled Blork. "Let go!"

The Thing that had him did not let go. In fact, it didn't even notice it had him. It was too busy picking food. It dropped Blork into the basket at its side, along with the other food it had picked, and walked on. Blork tried to climb out of the basket, but every time he got to the edge, the Thing dropped another juicy purple globe on his head.

At least the juice tasted good. Blork decided the globes must be some kind of fruit.

He was glad they weren't *vegetables*.

Since he couldn't get out, he decided to eat. He ate one fruit after another. Soon he had given himself a stomachache. As the basket bounced along at the Thing's side, Blork began to feel sicker and sicker.

"Let me out!" he cried.

The Thing ignored him.

After what seemed like hours, they came to a halt. Blork felt the basket being lifted, then turned over. "Yow!" he cried as he came rolling out along with all the purple fruit. Lunk came rolling out of another basket. Blork gulped. He was glad to see Lunk. But if the Things had picked a poodnoobie, they must be very strong.

He looked around. They were in a big room. Just then one of the Things noticed Blork. Looking puzzled, it walked over and picked him up. Another Thing picked up Lunk. They got in a big circle and began to jabber, until one Thing bellowed *"Skreehut!"* in a voice so loud Blork thought it would break his eardrums. All the other Things were quiet.

"Squat," said the Thing. The other Things mumbled and muttered for a while.

"Squat!" they said at last.

But none of them squatted. Blork wondered what was going on.

The Things walked out of the room, into a long hall made of stone. The hall went on and on. They walked and walked. At last they came to a big room. At one end of the room was a big throne.

Blork decided they must be in a castle.

A man sat on the throne. He was shorter than Blork, from the look of him. He had a very grumpy expression on his face.

"What is this?" cried the man.

Blork relaxed. At least the man spoke Standard Galactic. It would be good to have someone to talk to again.

"This is Blork," he said, pointing to himself.

"What were you doing in the royal gardens?"

"My poodnoobie and I were looking for food," said Blork. "We were hungry."

"No food!" cried the man. "All the food belongs to me, the Mighty Squat. And I don't share!"

Squat made a motion. The Thing that was carrying Blork put him down. The other Thing put Lunk down.

"Come here," said Squat. He had a crafty look in his eyes.

Blork swallowed. He walked toward Squat. The monarch jumped off his throne. He was indeed smaller than Blork. He looked Blork over carefully, poking and prodding him. He grabbed Blork's arms and pinched them.

"Yes," said Squat. "You'll do. You'll do very nicely."

"Do for what?" asked Blork.

"For a slave!"

Blork laughed. "That's ridiculous. Slavery is illegal."

"Not here it isn't," said Squat. "I make the rules here. And one of the rules is, if I want a slave, I get one."

"Well, it's not going to be me," said Blork. "Forget it!"

Squat looked at Blork as if he couldn't believe what he had just heard. "You dare disobey *me?*" he cried. "No one disobeys the Mighty Squat!"

Squat climbed back onto his throne. He

clenched his fists and began to shake. He let out a loud squawk.

Blork was curious. "What are you doing?" he asked.

"I'm having a tantrum, you fool!"

Blork laughed right out loud. "You call *that* a tantrum? Watch this!"

Blork had a tantrum. It was spectacular.

When he was done, Squat jumped off the throne. "That was fantastic!" he said. "Teach me how to do it."

"I will not," said Blork. "I have the greatest tantrums in the galaxy. Everyone says so. If I teach you, I won't be the best anymore."

"Oh, a stubborn one, eh?" said Squat. "Well, it won't do you any good. You'll change your mind soon enough."

He turned to the Things. "Take him away."

Two Things came to the front of the throne room. One picked up Blork. The other picked up Lunk. They carried them deep into the castle, threw them in a cell, and locked the door.

Blork was a prisoner, a slave of the Mighty Squat.

5

THINGS

The next morning a Thing came to Blork's cell and opened the door. It said something in Thing talk. Blork had no idea what the words meant. The Thing turned around and walked off.

Blork followed the Thing.

Lunk followed Blork.

After a while they came to a big room. Dozens of Things were sitting at long tables, eating breakfast. The Thing that had come to get Blork pointed to a place. Blork climbed onto a bench, then climbed back down.

He had no intention of eating the gooey

green mess on that plate! "It looks like scrambled boogers," he whispered to Lunk.

Lunk stared woefully at Blork. It was clear that he didn't care what the stuff on the plate looked like; he was one hungry poodnoobie. Blork slid the plate off the table and set it on the floor. Lunk made a happy chittering sound as he gobbled up the food. When he was done, he used all three tongues to lick the plate until it sparkled.

Blork went to the Thing that had led him here. "I don't eat that kind of stuff," he said loudly. "I want Sugar Blobs."

Sugar Blobs were Blork's favorite breakfast cereal.

"Eablach," said the Thing. It turned back to its breakfast.

Blork tugged on its arm. "I want some Sugar Blobs," he said more loudly.

The Thing ignored him.

"Sugar Blobs!" screamed Blork. "Sugar Blobs, Sugar Blobs, Sugar Blobs!"

The Thing stood up. Carefully it turned Blork around. Then it gave him a good swift kick in the pants.

Blork landed several feet away. This was too much. He opened his mouth for a tantrum and got the worst shock of his life. His tantrum power was gone!

Blork didn't know it, but when his tantrums had failed him three times—first over the D in geography, then over Lunk, and finally yesterday, when Squat had made him a slave—something inside him had been crushed. Now the tantrums just wouldn't come.

Blork was stunned. And furious. He got up, ready to rush back and pound the Thing that had kicked him. But when he looked around, he saw that all the Things were staring at him.

Not one of them looked friendly.

Blork decided he had better go back to his seat quietly. But before he could sit down, a bell rang.

The Things stood and marched out of the room. Blork stayed in his seat—until the Thing that had led him to breakfast made it clear that if he knew what was good for him, he would come along.

Blork followed the Things to a big cave underneath the castle. The Thing in charge of Blork handed him a bucket and a brush. Then it led him to a long hall.

"Grimble!" said the Thing.

"What?"

The Thing got down on its hands and knees and made scrubbing motions. Blork couldn't believe it. They wanted him to wash the floor! He threw down the brush, crossed his arms, and turned his back. "I don't do floors," he said.

The Thing gave him a swift kick in the pants.

Blork picked up the brush and started scrubbing.

He also made up his mind that he was going to get that Thing if it was the last thing he ever did.

The day wore on. Blork got very hungry. At last a bell rang. The Thing came to get him. Lunch didn't look any better than breakfast had, but Blork decided to eat it anyway. The Thing noticed that Blork was eating. It also noticed that there was nothing for Lunk to eat. It went and got a plate full of food and brought it to the poodnoobie.

Suddenly Blork was not as mad at the Thing as he had been.

That afternoon Blork had to feed the Snargs. These were strange creatures with long tentacles that lived in a cavern under the castle. Blork didn't like the job. It was scary.

By the time the supper bell rang, Blork was exhausted. He fell asleep with his head on his plate. A Thing picked him up and carried him to his cell. Lunk followed quietly behind. The Thing put Blork in his bed, pulled the covers over him, and sang a little song. Then it tiptoed out of the room.

Blork slept very soundly.

The next day was the same, and the next, except that Blork was starting to learn some words in Thing talk. He was not quite so mad now. But he still wanted to get Squat.

On the fourth night Blork was not so tired after supper. When the Things got up from the table, he went with them. They went into a big room lit by torches. They all sat down and began to sing. It was a strange song. The

Things had low, gravelly voices, and the rhythm was odd, almost frightening. Yet Blork found that he liked it.

Next, one of the Things got up and began to talk. From the looks on the faces of the other Things, he was telling a story. Blork listened carefully, but he could make no sense of it. Soon all the Things began laughing hysterically. Later in the story several of them began to cry.

Blork decided he had to learn their language.

After a while a couple of the Things began to nod. One or two stretched out on the floor and began to snore.

Lunk went over and poked his nose into a Thing's face, to see what the strange sound was. The Thing was snoring so hard it blew Lunk's ears backward like streamers.

Lunk looked puzzled. He nudged the Thing again. The Thing kissed him. Lunk came running back to Blork.

After a while Blork began to yawn, too. He put his arms around Lunk.

Minutes later they were both asleep.

After that, Blork slept in the big cave with the Things every night.

Blork discovered something interesting. The more Thing talk he learned, the easier it was to learn even more. He began to learn faster and faster. As he learned, he began to talk with the Things, even make friends with them. He decided that Things were all right. They told him stories. They sang him songs. They made him feel like he was one of them.

The only problem was, they would not put up with any brattiness. The minute Blork started to act like a brat, they gave him a good swift kick in the seat of his pants. Blork had already lost his tantrum power. Now he had to give up most of his bratty ways, too. They just weren't worth the pain.

He resented it. But the Things were so good and kind to him in every other way that he couldn't stay mad. He liked them, and he felt bad that they were slaves to Squat.

When he learned their history, he felt even worse.

It seemed Things were basically gentle creatures who did not know much about fighting. This was partly because they were so big that nothing much bothered them.

Then one day Squat had landed on their planet in his spaceship. He had a ray gun. He showed them what it could do by blasting a tree to smithereens. Then he said he was going to be their king, and they were to be his slaves.

The Things talked among themselves. They weren't sure they would go along with Squat.

Squat blew another tree to smithereens.

The Things decided they would go along with him after all.

It was Squat who had made them build the castle. It was Squat who made them work in the fields, and scrub the floors, and feed the

Snargs. It was Squat who kept them from dancing in the meadows, as Things were meant to do.

The Things did not like Squat. But they did not like to fight, either. And they were afraid of his gun.

Blork began to dislike Squat more and more.

One day Blork was put in the throne room to work. Squat was sitting on his throne, scowling at everything in sight. He did not look like he was king of anything.

Blork was given a small brush and told to polish Squat's toes. As he worked he got madder and madder.

After a while Squat called out to a big Thing standing nearby. It shambled over to the throne.

Blork recognized the Thing. It was the castle cook.

"I've made up my mind what I want for supper," said Squat.

The Thing grunted, which meant, "What?"

"That," said Squat with a smile.

Blork gasped. Squat was pointing at Lunk.

6

TANTRUMS

"That poodnoobie belongs to me!" cried Blork.

"So?"

"So I don't want you to eat him."

"Why not?"

"Because I love him!"

Squat laughed right out loud. "You can't possibly think that makes any difference to me! I couldn't care less."

Blork felt something begin to bubble up inside of him. It was a hot wave of anger at

Squat. He began to tremble. He began to shake. He felt himself get dizzy.

And then it erupted. His anger at being made a slave, at being forced to do nasty jobs, and most of all at Squat for thinking of harming Lunk, all came bursting out in one great rush. Blork had his tantrum power back, and now he put on one of the greatest tantrums of all time!

Squat climbed up on his throne to get out of the way. The Things backed up against the walls. The Snargs in the dungeons began to howl in fright.

Blork just rolled right on, kicking, screaming, and pounding the floor. He even pounded the walls. He gnashed his teeth. He turned blue in the face.

He bit the Mighty Squat on the toe.

The Things gasped. What would Squat do now?

But as Blork wound down, a greedy expression crossed Squat's face. "That was fantastic!" he cried. "Teach me to have a tantrum like that, and I will give you your freedom!"

Blork was sick of being a slave. He was

ready to teach Squat. But he had to be sure of one thing.

"Lunk, too?" he asked.

"Lunk, too."

"It's a deal!"

So the tantrum lessons began. Blork taught Squat every trick he knew—how to pound the floor without really hurting yourself; how to hold your breath until you turned blue (and when to let go so you wouldn't faint); how to turn red by clenching your neck muscles without getting a cramp. Blork also taught Squat how to pitch his screams so they were incredibly ear-piercing, and how to tighten his body so that it trembled like he was having a fit.

But something odd was happening. Blork had always been proud of his tantrum power. Now he didn't feel that way. In fact, watching Squat, he felt kind of sick.

Blork wasn't sure what was going on. He just wanted to finish giving Squat his lessons and get out.

Finally the day came when Blork had taught Squat everything he knew. "Well, that's it," he said. "I guess Lunk and I will be going now."

"Oh, no, you won't."

Blork stopped in his tracks. "What?"

"I said, 'Oh, no, you won't.' You're not going anywhere."

"But you promised . . ."

Squat waved his hand. "I don't keep promises."

"Well, you're keeping this one," said Blork. And he continued to walk out of the throne room.

"Stop!" cried Squat.

Blork didn't stop.

"Stop that brat!" yelled Squat, pointing to the nearest Thing. "Grab that poodnoobie!"

The Thing didn't move.

"Somebody stop them!" cried Squat.

No one moved.

Squat couldn't believe it. He began to tremble. He began to shake. And then he let loose with one of the most fearsome tantrums in the history of the galaxy.

Blork turned around to watch. He thought he was going to throw up. Squat was disgusting.

And he learned it all from me! thought Blork in horror. He began to think. He thought about how cranky Squat was.

He thought about himself.

He thought about how demanding Squat was.

He thought about himself.

He thought about how basically disgusting Squat was.

He thought about himself.

He was not very happy.

Meanwhile, Squat was getting really wound up. He was bouncing across on the floor, screaming and foaming at the mouth, changing color every ten seconds.

Blork looked past Squat toward the throne. He saw the ray gun, sitting in its usual place! Running past Squat, he snatched up the gun. "Here!" he cried, tossing it to a Thing. "Catch!"

The Thing caught the gun. For a moment it stared at it with a puzzled expression on its face. Then it realized what Blork had done. It understood the chance.

Making an awful face, the Thing bit the gun in half.

The crunching noise made Squat stop his tantrum for a second. But when he saw what the Thing had done, he started up again, worse than ever.

The Chief Thing went over to Squat and picked him up.

"Enough is enough," said the Thing. It carried Squat to the nearest window, held him over the edge, and let go. They could hear Squat screaming and cursing all the way down to the moat. Then they heard a huge splash.

Blork ran to the window. Looking down, he saw Squat climb out of the moat. The little man looked up and shook his fist at the castle. "If that's the way you're going to be, I don't want to play anymore!" he cried. "I'm going home!"

Blork looked at the Things. The Things looked at Blork.

They all began to laugh.

That night they had a big party in the castle. The Things ate and sang and told stories late into the night.

Blork enjoyed the celebration. But part of him was sad. At first he couldn't figure it out.

The Things were wonderful. But they weren't like he was. Blork was lonesome for his own kind. As much as he liked it here with the Things, Splat was his home.

Finally the whole truth hit him. He was homesick.

He had to go back.

The next morning Blork got ready to leave. The Things helped him load the rocket with food. They gave him some presents: a warm blanket, a wooden plaque with half of Squat's ray gun on it, and a stone carving of a Thing feeding a Snarg.

Blork put the gifts carefully into the ship.

"Good-bye, Blork," said the Chief Thing, his voice sounding like two stones grinding together. "We will miss you."

Blork smiled sadly. "I will miss you, too," he said. Then he put Lunk in the rocket car, closed the door behind him, and got ready to blast off.

Now only one thing was bothering Blork.

Which way was home?

"I guess we'll just have to look for it," he said to Lunk. Pushing forward on the accelerator, he lifted off from the planet of the Things.

He decided to orbit it once, so he could swoop down and wave a final farewell. But halfway around the planet Blork pulled back on the accelerator so fast they almost fell out of the sky.

He couldn't believe his eyes.

7

HOME

Blork looked down and laughed so hard that tears rolled down his face. When he had gotten turned around in space, he had gotten *really* turned around. He had been on the Unexplored Zone of Splat all this time. He just hadn't recognized the planet's far side.

He sighed. No wonder Modra Ploogsik had given him that D in geography!

Soon Blork was flying over his own colony. It felt good to be home.

Or did it? Suddenly Blork sobered up. He

was still in a lot of trouble down there. But where else could he go? If his recent adventures were any indication, one place was no better than another—and might be worse.

Besides, for better or worse, this *was* home. He understood that now. He would just have to do the best he could to straighten things out. But one thing was still certain: He wouldn't let anything happen to Lunk.

Slowing the ship, Blork began to look for the Block 78 Child House. Finally he spotted it.

Working carefully, he made a perfect landing on the roof.

He unstrapped Lunk. Boy and poodnoobie climbed out of the ship and walked to the door that led down into the building. Just as they reached it, the door flew open and out stormed the Childkeeper.

"What are you doing here?" it yelled. "This roof is for private . . ." The Childkeeper stopped in midsentence. Its dials began to spin. Then, using a completely different voice, it cried, "Blork! Where have you been?"

Before Blork could answer, the Childkeeper

rolled over and scratched Lunk behind the ears. "Nice to see you, boy," it said.

Blork looked at the Childkeeper in surprise. He had not expected it to be glad to see Lunk.

An hour later Blork and the Childkeeper went to see Modra Ploogsik.

"Blork!" cried the teacher when she saw him walk through the door. "Where have you been all these weeks? I've been worried sick!"

"It's a long story," said Blork, trying to hide his surprise that Modra Ploogsik had been worried about him. "Right now I've come to see you about Lunk. I want to know if you will call off the Big Pest Squad."

At the mention of Lunk's name Modra Ploogsik's jaw began to clench. An angry fire glimmered in her eye. "I'm afraid that is not possible, Blork," she said firmly. "That pood-noobie is a menace."

Blork couldn't believe it. She still wanted to have Lunk turned into dust! Blork was furious. He began to shake. His insides boiled. He could feel a mighty tantrum coming!

Then he thought of Squat and how disgusting he was. He felt sick. The tantrum seemed to curl up and go away.

Blork took a deep breath. "I'm very sorry for the damage Lunk caused," he said. "But it wasn't really his fault. It was mine. I will be glad to work to make it up."

Modra Ploogsik fell off her chair.

The Childkeeper put its hand on Blork's

forehead. "Is it really you, Blork?" it asked in concern. "Do you feel all right?"

"I don't feel good at all," replied Blork. "I am very worried about Lunk. I don't want him to be hurt because of me."

Modra Ploogsik got up. She was quiet for a moment. "Do you really feel that way?" she finally asked.

"Oh, I do, I do!" cried Blork.

"Then I think we can figure something out. But it will mean a lot of hard work."

"It can't be worse than feeding Snargs."

"What?"

"Nothing. When do you want me to start?"

"Tomorrow will be soon enough," said the teacher. "Right now I want you to tell me where you have been."

So Blork told his adventures to Modra Ploogsik and the Childkeeper. Then he had to take the rocket back to the Big Pest Squad. He was in a lot of trouble there, too. But careful, patient apologies—along with some help from the Childkeeper—cleared that up.

At last they headed back for the Block 78 Child House.

Blork ran up the stairs. "Hey, Lunk!" he cried. "I'm home!"

He threw open the door to his room.

Lunk came bounding out.

Badoom! Badoom! Badoom!

"Ah, the patter of tiny feet," said the Childkeeper with a sigh, as it rolled off to look for some aspirin.

Lunk licked Blork's face with all three tongues at once.

About the Author and the Illustrator

BRUCE COVILLE was born in Syracuse, New York. He grew up in a rural area north of the city, around the corner from his grandparents' dairy farm. In the years before he was able to make his living full-time as a writer, Bruce was, among other things, a gravedigger, a toymaker, a magazine editor, and a door-to-door salesman. He loves reading, musical theater, and being outdoors.

In addition to more than sixty books for young readers, Bruce has written poems, plays, short stories, newspaper articles, thousands of letters, and several years' worth of journal entries.

Some of Bruce's best-known books are *My Teacher Is an Alien*, *Goblins in the Castle*, and *Aliens Ate My Homework*.

KATHERINE COVILLE is a self-taught artist who is known for her ability to combine finely detailed drawings with a deliciously wacky sense of humor. She is also a toymaker, specializing in creatures hitherto unseen on this planet. Her other collaborations with Bruce Coville include *The Monster's Ring*, *The Foolish Giant*, *Sarah's Unicorn*, *Goblins in the Castle*, *Aliens Ate My Homework*, and the *Space Brat* series.

The Covilles live in a brick house in Syracuse along with their youngest child, three cats, and a jet-powered Norwegian elkhound named Thor.